To Know the Sea

Written by
Frances Gilbert

Illustrated by
Rhett Ransom Pennell

Greene Bark Press, Inc.

Publisher's Catalog-in-Publication
(Provided by Quality Books Inc.)
Gilbert, Frances
To Know the Sea / written by Frances Gilbert;
illustrated by Rhett Ransom Pennell. -- 1st ed.

p. cm.
SUMMARY: A young princess is unhappy until she finds a way
to know the sea.
LCCN: 00-132340
ISBN: 1-88085-160-1

1. Princesses--Juvenile fiction. 2. Ocean--Juvenile fiction.
I. Pennell, Rhett Ransom. II. Title

PZ7.G5534Kno 2000   [E]
                           QBIOO-466

For David and Jeremy
who have the sea in their hearts
and
for Peter
-- F. G.

For Margaret
who teaches me to swim farther
and enjoy the waves.
-- R. R. P.

High in a faraway mountain kingdom there was trouble....

Isola, the littlest princess, was having a tantrum.
She flounced and she stamped.
She screamed and she wailed.
She would not clean her room, she would not eat her veggies,
and she refused to wear her tiara.

There was consternation throughout the court.
The King took to his bed, "You handle it, my dear," he said.
The distraught Queen rushed around the palace asking advice
while the Princess shrieked and flailed.

"There's no doing
anything with her,"
said the Queen.

"Send her to bed,"
hissed her six sisters.

"Bread and water for a week,"
murmured the court ladies.

"Put her in the dungeon," growled
the old advisors.
"Outrageous behavior!" they
trumpeted together.

But one old granny said quietly,
"Why don't you ask her what she
wants?"

The shrieking stopped. The princess took a breath.

"I want...

"I want...

"I want to know the sea," she announced.

"Know the sea?" chorused the sisters, the ladies, and the advisors.
"No one knows the sea. No one from here has ever *been* to the sea.
It's ridiculous, impossible...forget about it!"

Isola was inconsolable.
She drooped and dragged about the palace.
She wouldn't practice her reading or do her math, and she flung away her tiara.
She sobbed for the sea
and wept herself wretched.

"This can't go on," said the King to the Queen, from his bed.
"See about it, my dear, bring her the sea."
The Queen had no idea how this could be done
but she posted notices throughout the realm.
"A Reward - To The First One To Bring The Sea To The Littlest Princess."

Down in the valleys, across the plains, and all the long way to the coast,
the people buzzed and chattered.
How could anyone bring the sea all the way inland to the Princess?
Wasn't the sea a wild thing, capricious and unruly?
It couldn't be done.

Eventually one young man thought of a way.
"No need to bring the whole ocean," he decided.
"I will bring her the taste of the sea and the smell of the sea."
So he hauled a great jar of sea water, strapped it onto his horse, and off he galloped
to bring the sea to the Princess in her distant home.

He journeyed for days over rough ground in the hot sun.
"I am bringing the sea to the Princess," he called as he passed.
But the farther he went, the more sea water sloshed and splashed out of the jar.
The sun's heat evaporated the water left inside
until he arrived at the palace with an empty, smelly, sea-weedy jar.

"Pee-ew!" screamed the six sisters holding their noses. "Take it away."
The littlest princess was very disappointed
but she thanked the wet and salty young man.
She hung the seaweed on the palace wall,
climbed up to the palace turrets, and watched for the sea to come to her.

A second young man watching the sea run up onto the beaches thought,
"I will make the sea follow me."
So he dug a channel, across the plains and through the valley,
and the sea followed him; running forward, rolling along behind him,
singing it's watery, lapping song.

"I am bringing the sea to the Princess," he called
as he raced inland, digging as fast as he could.
But the farther he went up the mountains the more the sea fell behind
(for no one can make the sea run uphill),
and he arrived at the palace with an empty, dusty, dirty ditch.

"Pshaw!" said the ladies of the court, covering their mouths, "Fill it in."
The littlest princess was very disappointed
but she thanked the sweaty, dusty young man,
planted lilies in the ditch,
and hid in the garden to imagine the sea's songs in her heart.

A third young man had a better idea.
"No need for all this mess and dirt," he decided,
"I will bring the sea sound in a shell to calm her nerves."
So he sought out a beautifully twirled shell with a pinky pearly inside,
put it in his pocket and set off for the palace.

"I am bringing the sea to the Princess," he cried
as he strode through the villages.
But alas, no one had told the young man that sea creatures
often make their homes in spare shells,
and when the princess lifted the shell...

...out rushed a little crab and nipped her ear!

"Away with him," shrieked the advisors
before the Princess could even thank him.
The guards bundled him out of the palace and sent him on his way.

The Princess put the shell and the little crab in a bowl in her bathroom
and went to sit by the moat to watch and wait.

For many months, no one else tried to bring the sea to the Princess.
Sometimes when she was alone in one of the great halls of the palace
she would close her eyes to feel the rolling sea under her feet.
She strained to hear, faint and far away, the swish of the waves
and every so often she would feel the pull of the tides and weep.

"You will have to do something, my dear," said the King to the Queen,
"this is very trying on my nerves."
"Isola," said the Queen, "this is too big a dream.
Look around you. Consider your duties here."
"Mother," said Isola, "the sea calls me. I must know the sea."

Just then a figure appeared toiling up the mountain slope
following the lily path where the sea could not run.
It was an old man, wearing a blue sweater and big boots
and carrying a long canvas pack on his back.
He came through the palace gate and up to the Princess.

"I am Peter," he said, "and I have brought you the sea."
Isola looked at his steady eyes and old brown face.
"Where is it?" she cried.

"The sea is in my heart,"
replied Peter, "and here
in my pack."

He up-ended his pack
and out tumbled all
manner of books.

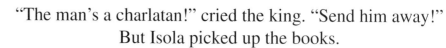

"The man's a charlatan!" cried the king. "Send him away!"
But Isola picked up the books.
"Why," she said, "these are all stories about the sea."
"Yes," said Peter, "and math, geography and astronomy.
Without these things no one can understand the sea."

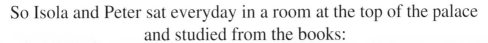

So Isola and Peter sat everyday in a room at the top of the palace
and studied from the books:
latitude and longitude, trade winds and doldrums, tides and currents,
the ebb and flow of histories on the seas, the creatures in its depths.
All the while, Peter spun tales of his voyages.

r. L. oceanus, ...
river supposed to enco...
The whole body of salt wate...
fourths of the surface of the ...
...at sea. The average ...

Gradually, Isola began to know the sea,
the seamless skin that holds our world together.
She felt its heaving angry moods, its wild and rolling chase,
and its sunny sparkling face.
She understood that the sea gives and takes according to its own laws.

"Now I am ready," she said. "Now I am ready to meet the sea."
So Peter and Isola came down from the mountains,

and crossed the valleys and plains to the coast.

There Isola sold her tiara and
bought a sturdy little boat
which she named
"The Isola Marina."

With Isola as captain and Peter as first mate
the Isola Marina ventured far and wide,
crossing the boundless open seas, borne by the winds and tides...

You may catch a glimpse of them sometimes when your heart opens
and your soul is free to know the sea.